W9-ART-847

011253

E

$

DATE DUE			
MAR 0 8 2004			
OCT 1 3 2004			
NOV 0 8 2004			

MAY
JUN
OCT
NOV
DEC
J MA

1999
1999
1999
2000
2001
2000
2001

Kiki's New Sister

STORY AND PICTURES
BY
Jennifer Barrett

A BANTAM LITTLE ROOSTER BOOK

NEW YORK · TORONTO · LONDON · SYDNEY · AUCKLAND

KIKI'S NEW SISTER

A Bantam Little Rooster Book / March 1992

Little Rooster.is a trademark of Bantam Books, a division of
Bantam Doubleday Dell Publishing Group, Inc.

Library of Congress Cataloging-in-Publication Data
Barrett, Jennifer.
Kiki's new sister / written and illustrated by Jennifer Barrett.
p. cm.
"A Bantam little rooster book."
Summary: When Kiki suggests sending her new baby sister back to the hospital, her parents
wisely suggest Kiki spend more time helping care for the baby before making a decision.
ISBN 0-553-07567-5
1. Dinosaurs—Fiction. [1. Babies—Fiction. 2. Sisters—Fiction.] I. Title.
PZ7.B27515Ki   1992
[E]–dc20
91-7303
CIP
AC

Published simultaneously in the United States and Canada

Bantam Books are published by Bantam Books, a division of Bantam Doubleday Dell Publishing
Group, Inc. Its trademark, consisting of the words "Bantam Books" and the portrayal of a rooster,
is Registered in U.S. Patent and Trademark Office and in other countries. Marca Registrada.
Bantam Books, 666 Fifth Avenue, New York, New York 10103.

PRINTED IN ITALY

NIL   0 9 8 7 6 5 4 3 2 1

For Deborah
a generous teacher
and
Sally, who helped make it possible

Kiki had a new baby sister.

"I like her," Kiki said at first.
The baby slept a lot and didn't bother anyone . . .

only sometimes she smelled.

But soon the baby started staying awake longer
and screaming for no reason.
"Tell her to be quiet!" Kiki cried. "She's not even
saying anything!"

It got worse.

At night the baby fussed and cried, keeping everyone awake.

In the morning Kiki's parents were grouchy and breakfast wasn't fun anymore.

Then the baby chewed Kiki's toys and made
messes everywhere. She was even noisy during
Kiki's favorite show.

This baby is awful! Kiki thought. She decided to talk to her parents and made a careful plan of what to say.

But whenever she got ready to say it, they were too busy

feeding the baby,

changing her,

playing with her,

or bathing her.

Finally her mother asked, "Kiki, what's wrong?"

But all Kiki could say was, "Nothing."

One morning Kiki woke up early.
She went into her parents' room and climbed onto
their bed.

"I want to know," Kiki said, "if we are keeping this baby forever. Maybe we should bring her back to the hospital."

Her parents looked at each other.
"Maybe," her father said, "we can all decide what
to do."
"Yes," her mother agreed. "But before you make a
decision, you should spend some extra time with
the baby so you are sure that you make the right
choice."

"Well . . ." said Kiki, "all right."

That day Kiki helped her parents

feed the baby,

change her,

play with her,

and bathe her.

She helped get the baby ready for bed and kissed
her good night.

"So?" her mother said. "What do you think?
Should we keep her?"

"She's still too noisy sometimes," said Kiki.
"She can be noisy," her father agreed.
"And she makes a lot of messes and
takes a lot of our time."
"She does," her mother said.
"But I think she likes us," Kiki said, "and she's fun
to play with sometimes. We can
probably teach her to be quieter
and not so messy."
"We probably can," said her father.

"So I think for now we should keep her," Kiki decided.
Her parents smiled. "So do we," they said.

It was bedtime, so Kiki's father carried her
upstairs.

"This baby is lucky to be in our family," Kiki said.
"And we are lucky to have you," said her mother.
They tucked her in and gave her a kiss.
"Good night, Kiki," they said.

But Kiki didn't answer. She had already fallen asleep.